P9-EKY-589

![Mike the Knight logo] MiKE THE KNIGHT

The Jewel of Glendragon

adapted by Cordelia Evans

based on the screenplay written by Simon Nicholson

Ready-to-Read

Simon Spotlight

New York   London   Toronto   Sydney   New Delhi

SIMON SPOTLIGHT
An imprint of Simon & Schuster Children's Publishing Division
1230 Avenue of the Americas, New York, New York 10020

For information about special discounts for bulk purchases, please contact Simon & Schuster
Special Sales at 1-866-506-1949 or business@simonandschuster.com.
The Simon & Schuster Speakers Bureau can bring authors to your live event. For more information
or to book an event contact the Simon & Schuster Speakers Bureau at 1-866-248-3049 or visit our
website at www.simonspeakers.com.
Manufactured in the United States of America 0713 LAK
First Edition 10 9 8 7 6 5 4 3 2 1
ISBN 978-1-4424-8634-8 (pbk)
ISBN 978-1-4424-8635-5 (hc)
ISBN 978-1-4424-8636-2 (eBook)

One day Mike was playing

hide-and-seek with

Sparkie and Squirt.

"Mike," said Queen Martha. "The Jewel of Glendragon has come loose from my crown. Can you help me?"

"Of course!" said Mike.
"I will take it to
Mr. Blacksmith. He will
fix it!"

On the way to see
Mr. Blacksmith they ran
into Mrs. Piecrust.
She was making cherry pies.

"So many people want cherry pies for dessert tonight!" said Mrs. Piecrust. "Will you help me make them?"

"Of course," said Mike.

"But what will I do

with the crown?"

"Put it on your head,"

said Squirt.

"It will be safe there."

Soon the pies were done.

"Thank you,"

said Mrs. Piecrust.

Mike and the dragons set off

to see Mr. Blacksmith.

But when they arrived,

they discovered something

awful:

The Jewel of Glendragon

was no longer in the crown!

"Where could it be?"

asked Sparkie.

"What if it fell into a pie?"

asked Squirt.

Mike had an idea.

"Sparkie can eat the pies to find the jewel!" said Mike.

Sparkie liked that idea!

He loved cherry pie.

They went to the first house
where Mrs. Piecrust had
delivered a pie.
No one was home.

Sparkie ate the pie.

There was no jewel.

No one was home at the second house where Mrs. Piecrust had delivered a pie.

Sparkie ate the pie.

There was still no jewel.

Then Mr. Shepherd

came home.

"Sparkie, why did you eat

my pie?" he asked.

"It is my fault," said Mike.

"We were looking for the

Jewel of Glendragon.

I will make you a new pie."

After they made new pies,

Mike and his dragon friends

went home to tell

Queen Martha

what had happened.

"I am sad that you lost the jewel, but the important thing is that you told me. Now let's have some pie to cheer up."

As Mike cut into the pie,
the knife hit something hard.

"The Jewel of Glendragon!"

Mike said.

"We found it!"

Everyone cheered.
"Now, who would like the
first slice of pie?"
asked Mike.

"Not me," said Sparkie.
"I think I have had
enough pie for one day!"